D0179866

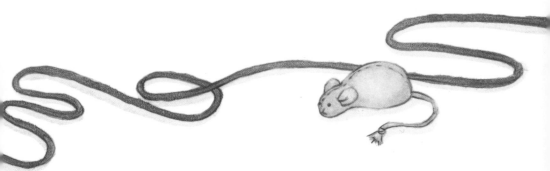

In memory of our cat Dickens
—L.M.S.

To Rob and Cyndi
—S.K.H.

Mittens Text copyright © 2006 by Lola M. Schaefer Illustrations copyright © 2006 by Susan Kathleen Hartung All rights reserved. No part of this book may be used or reproduced in any manner whatsoever without written permission except in the case of brief quotations embodied in critical articles and reviews. Manufactured in China. For information address HarperCollins Children's Books, a division of HarperCollins Publishers, 195 Broadway, New York, NY 10007. www.harpercollinschildrens.com

Library of Congress Cataloging-in-Publication Data
Schaefer, Lola M., date Mittens / story by Lola M. Schaefer ; pictures by Susan Kathleen Hartung.— 1st ed.
   p.   cm. — (My first I can read book)
  Summary: Nick helps Mittens the kitten adjust to life in a new home.
  ISBN-13: 978-0-06-054659-5 (trade bdg.) ISBN-10: 0-06-054659-X (trade bdg.)
  ISBN-13: 978-0-06-054660-1 (lib. bdg.) ISBN-10: 0-06-054660-3 (lib. bdg.)
  ISBN-13: 978-0-06-054661-8 (pbk.) ISBN-10: 0-06-054661-1 (pbk.)
   [1. Cats—Fiction. 2. Animals—Infancy—Fiction.] I. Hartung, Susan Kathleen, ill. II. Title. III. Series.
PZ7.S33233Mit 2006
[E]—dc22   2005019485

15 16 SCP 10 9 8 7 6 5 4
❖

Mittens

story by **Lola M. Schaefer**

pictures by **Susan Kathleen Hartung**

HarperCollins*Publishers*

Nick has a new kitten.

His name is Mittens.

"Mittens, this is
your new home," says Nick.

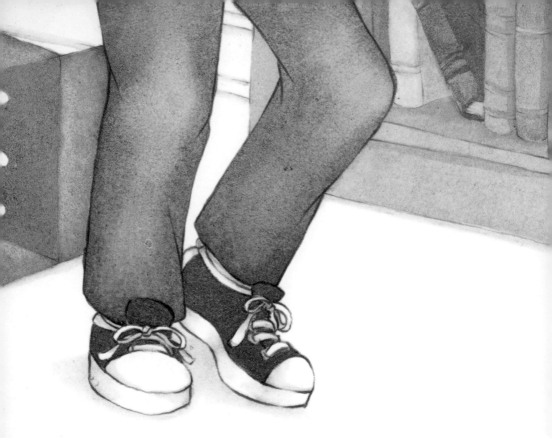

Mittens looks around.

Everything is new and big!

Mittens is scared.

Mittens wants a hiding place.
He wants a small place
just for him.

Zoom!

Mittens runs out of the room.

Zoom!

Mittens runs behind the T.V.

It is too loud.

Zoom!

Mittens runs under the sofa.

It is too dark.

Zoom!

Mittens runs down the hall
and under a bed.

This is it!

Mittens has a hiding place.

He has a small place
just for him.

15

But everything is still new.

Mittens is still scared!

Mittens cries, "Meow!"

"Mittens, where are you?"
calls Nick.

"Meow! Meow! Meow!"

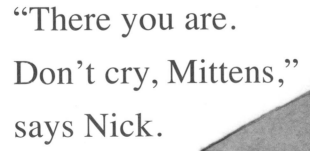

"There you are.
Don't cry, Mittens,"
says Nick.

19

Nick lies down.

"You are safe now," says Nick.

"I will take care of you."

Mittens moves toward Nick.
"I will be your friend,"
says Nick.

Mittens comes closer.

Nick waits.

Mittens curls up next to Nick.

"Welcome home, Mittens,"
says Nick.

Purrrrrr.

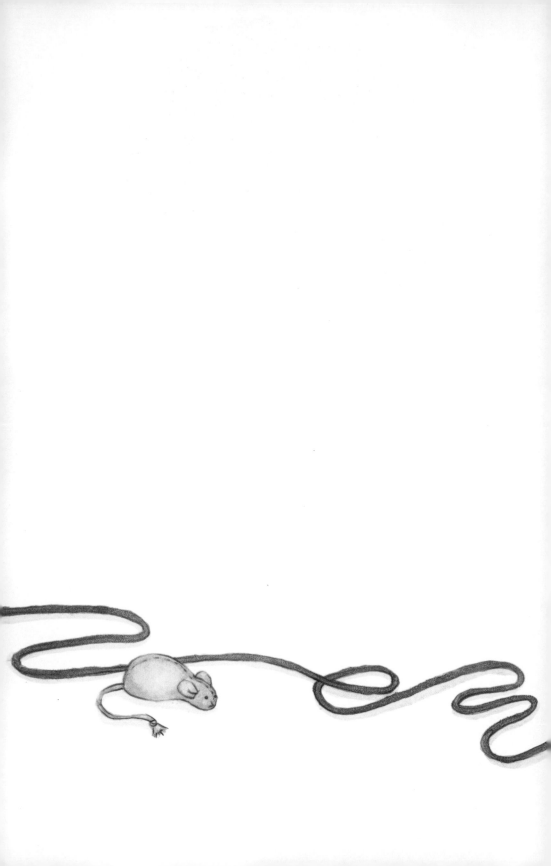